SESAME STREET

SESAME STREET'S MOTHER GOOSE RHYMES

By Constance Allen
Illustrated by Maggie Swanson

A SESAME STREET/GOLDEN BOOK
Published by Western Publishing Company, Inc.,
in conjunction with Children's Television Workshop.

Library of Congress Catalog Card Number: 92-72513 ISBN: 0-307-30122-2 MCMXCV

This educational book was created in cooperation with Children's Television Workshop, producers of SESAME STREET. Children do not have to watch the television show to benefit from this book. Workshop revenues from this product will be used to help support CTW educational projects.

Little Bo-Peep was counting sheep
but forgot what comes after ten.
The Count cried, "It's clear! Eleven, my dear!
And now let us count them again!"

Pat-a-cake, pat-a-cake, baker's man,
make lots of cakes as fast as you can.
Mix them and pour them,
and bake till they're through.
Then GOBBLE them up!
Pan delicious, too!

Old Mother Hubbard bounced to the cupboard
to find something starting with B.
"Oh, boy!" she said. "Here's a basket of bread!
What a beautiful breakfast for me!"

Peter Piper proudly polished paper clips.
How many paper clips did Peter Piper polish?
Peter Piper pointed at the pile.
"Plenty!" said Peter Piper proudly.

Little Jack Horner sat in a corner,
eating his anchovy pie.
A bird came to play,
Jack yelled, "Go away!"
and said, "What a good grouch am I!"

Little Miss Muffet sat on a tuffet,
eating a bowl of stew.
When a very big spider
sat down right beside her,
she said, "There is plenty for you!"

Hickory, dickory, dock.
The bird climbed up the clock!
When the clock struck two,
he cried, "CUCK-OO!
I'm the loudest clock on the block!"

Grundgetta, Grundgetta, where have you been?
"I took the jalopy out for a spin!"
Grundgetta, Grundgetta, where did you go?
"I went to the dump! Who wants to know?"

Rain, rain, go away,
great big monsters want to play.
Not tomorrow, pal. Today.

Old King Cole was a merry old soul,
for he only ate healthy food.
He called for his bread, and he called
for his cheese,
and he called for his fruit, nicely stewed.

Jack be nimble,
Jack be fast,
Jack is first,
and I am last.

JACK

Hey, diddle, diddle,
the Twiddlebugs fiddle,
and Gladys moos at the moon.
Barkley barks to see such sport,
and the grouch bangs his can with a spoon!

Sing a song of sixes,
six monsters do a dance,
six monsters with suspenders
holding up their pants.

Look above their heads
and count what you see there.
Six silly hats!
Now what a thing to wear!

Prairie had a little lamb
whose fleece was white as snow.
Her cow was brown, her dog was gray,
her baby chick was yellow.

One friend had shaggy purple fur,
the other friend was blue,
and everywhere the three friends went,
the pets would follow, too!

Twinkle, twinkle, little star,
Elmo wonders what you are.
Far away, up in the sky,
glinting like a firefly.
Twinkle, twinkle, in the air,
Elmo waves at you up there.